I0782223

Jim:
For his wife and kids, and he would like to issue an apology to his future grandkids. The world is nigh.

Michael:
For Sauda, with whom every minute spent is vitally important.

A Madness Heart Press Publication

Madness Heart Press
2006 Idlewilde Run Dr.
Austin, Texas 78744

This is a work of fiction. Names, characters, places, and incidents either are the product of the author's imagination or are used fictitiously. Any resemblance to actual persons, living or dead, events, or locales is entirely coincidental.

First Edition
ISBN: 978-1-955745-32-1
www.madnessheart.press

THE
LAST
5
minutes
Of
The
HUMAN RACE
Written by Michael Allen Rose
Illustrated by Jim Agpalza

A is for Apocalyptic

I saw the last five minutes of the human race. An **apocalyptic** war was in full swing. This was a war like none the world had ever seen. It made the very concept of a world war seem indescribably quaint. The most technologically developed countries had already long fallen to ash and ruin; their cities, dust; their people, bones. And yet still, the algorithms that drove the engines of war fought on despite there being nobody left to fight for. Secondary, then tertiary countries fell before the ceaseless nuclear onslaught. Anywhere that had been able to strike back had been struck first. I saw a remote village deep in the jungle, the last refuge of the human race, a tribe uncontacted by those who had built these weapons of mass destruction, on their own and better off for it. They sat in a large circle, those who remained. They spoke of how the stars in the sky had been moving in unfamiliar patterns, streaks of light blazing crimson scars across the surface of the sky. Night was no longer dark, with the heavens holding the strange glow of fire and smoke on such a scale that few corners of the Earth remained untouched. Only this place, this tiny cradle of the species, this last desperate hope. One star shone brighter than the others. An arc of red followed it, barely visible. An errant shot, one small mistake in the mathematics of devastation, this payload would be delivered to this accidental target. No military or economic significance, so it hadn't even been programmed into the endless cycle of rockets fired skyward, but the humans all watched as the star grew endlessly brighter, coming to meet them. A falling star. A mystery. An unfathomable gift from civilizations already dead. As it impacted, the ground shook, and then everything was consumed by fire in the last village.

B is for Baby

I saw the last five minutes of the human race. I was in a cave, watching a dead body, a young woman, naked, alone, and as I watched, something slid out of her. A **baby**. The last baby. I looked around, desperately trying to take in some detail that would help put this scene into context. The infant squirmed, helpless. It was the wrong color. It was a shade of blue, choking on air that, for some reason, was poison to its small body. As it tried to take a breath, I found myself breathing for it, willing my lungs to somehow transfer their power into this final vessel of what it meant to be human. I breathed in and out, mediating, ventilating, directing my every thought to making the tiny creature's lungs inflate, to fight for a chance, for five more minutes of life, but I could do nothing, and it died—we died—in darkness, alone.

I saw the last five minutes of the human race. I was in a cave, watching a dead body, a young woman, naked, alone, and as I watched, something slid out of her. A **baby**. The last baby. I looked around, desperately trying to take in some detail that would help put this scene into context. The infant squirmed, helpless. It was the wrong color. It was a shade of blue, choking on air that for some reason, was poison to its small body. As it tried to take a breath, I found myself breathing for it, willing my lungs to somehow transfer their power into this final vessel of what it meant to be human. I breathed in and out, mediating, ventilating, directing my every thought to making the tiny creature's lungs inflate, to fight for a chance, for five more minutes of life, but I could do nothing, and it died - we died - in darkness, alone.

C is for Cage

I saw the last five minutes of the human race. It was a cage of some kind, of some material I could not recognize. In the cage was a man, naked and afraid. He looked up, and although I knew he could not see me—because only an ephemeral part of me was there—I flinched at his uncomprehending gaze. A portal opened, and two beings entered, vaguely humanoid but taller, with larger brains. It unsettled me to look at them; they inhabited an uncanny valley nobody was prepared for. Both had what appeared to be metal parts embedded in their skin. Their anatomy was so similar to our own but yet stretched, distorted, alien. I thought about the concept of the uncanny valley and felt a creeping dread. The tingles up my spine meant that at one point in the evolution of the human race, there must have been something that looked very close to human but was dangerously not human. The hackles raised on my neck were a survival mechanism hard-coded into our biology screaming, "Beware, this looks like one of you, but do not be fooled." One of the creatures began to hum, and the other produced a silicon needle from within a pouch. They cornered the man, who was trembling. They approached him like one would approach a terrified animal, with what could only be described as compassion. One of the tall beings placed his hand on the man's head, and the other carefully pulled back the hair on the nape of the man's neck and applied pressure with the needle. The beings stroked the man's hair and softly held him as he slowly began to close his eyes. After a few moments, he seemed to fall asleep, and slowly, his chest, which had been moving up and down rapidly, came to an inevitable halt. The otherworldly veterinarians looked up and saw me through whatever veil I was behind, somehow peering through time and space. They simply stared, as though waiting for me to arrive for my own palliative care.

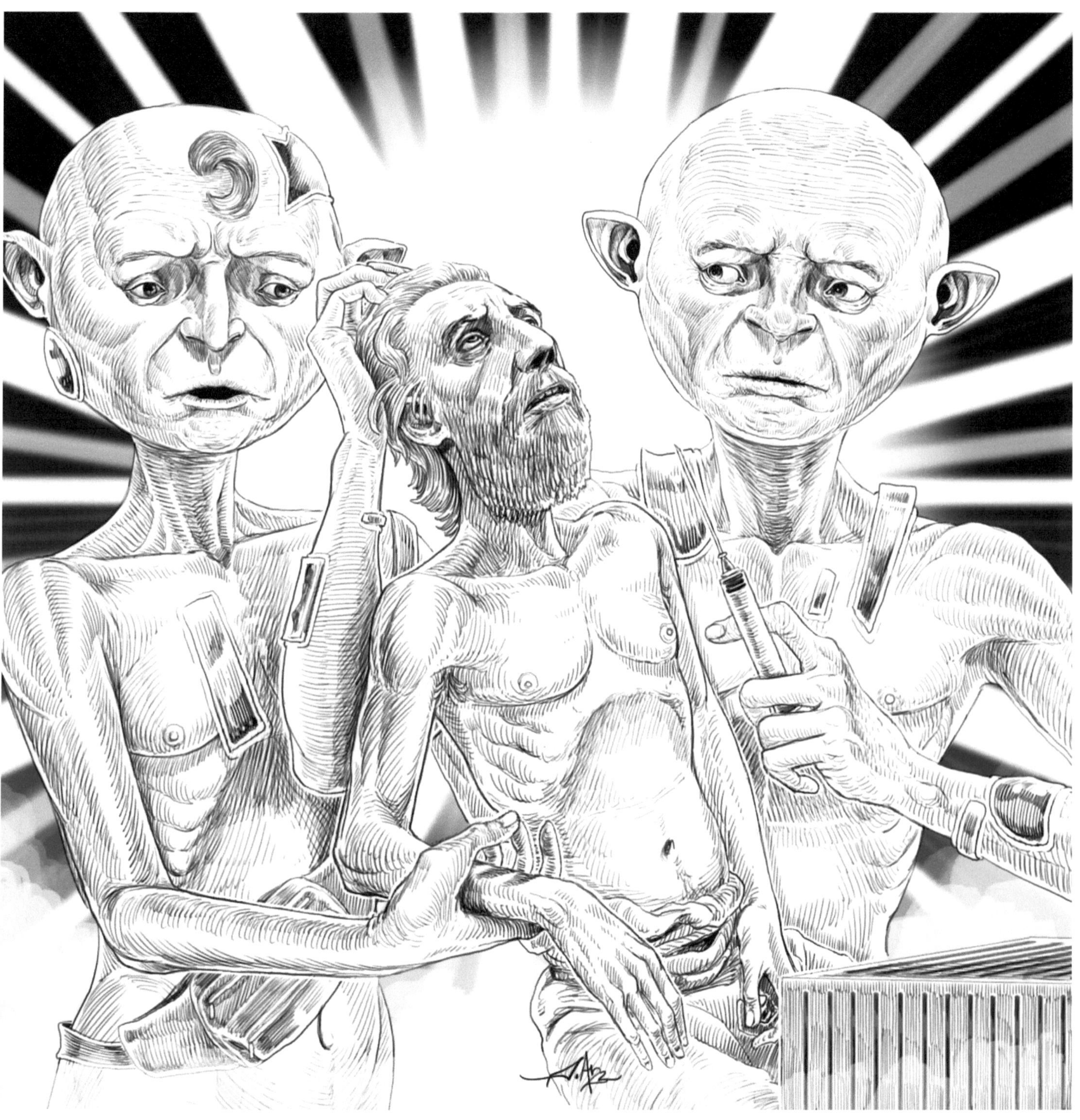

D is for Darkness

I saw the last five minutes of the human race. Actually, that's a lie; I was there, but I saw nothing. The Earth was covered in darkness. A final and impenetrable void, like death itself. There were no stars in the sky. No moon. No sun. The air was freezing cold, a cold beyond anything I'd ever felt before, penetrating the thickest layers of clothing. I waited there, in the darkness, standing, listening, hearing distant echoes of unfamiliar sounds. I strained to hear anything recognizable: the howl of a wolf, a bird scrounging for food, a voice, a shifting of the Earth. But I couldn't understand anything I heard. Distant clangs, like metal on metal. Scratching from under the ground. Then, finally, when my time was nearly up, in the quietest of voices, I heard one single word coming from somewhere far away. One last word, pregnant with meaning, gasped out along with a death rattle. I turned the word over and over in my mind and pondered what it might have meant. What legacy it had tried to leave with me. I wondered if meaning was something that could even be found. Then, the silence became suddenly much deeper.

I saw the last five minutes of the human race. Actually, that's a lie; I was there, but I saw nothing. The Earth was covered in darkness. A final and impenetrable void, like itself. There were no stars in the sky. No moon. No sun. The air was freezing cold, a cold beyond anything I'd ever felt before, penetrating the thickest layers of clothing. I waited there, in the darkness, standing, listening, hearing distant echoes of unfamiliar sounds. I strained to hear anything recognizable: the howl of a wolf, a bird scrounging for food, a voice, a shifting of the Earth. But I couldn't understand anything I heard. Distant clangs, like metal on metal. Scratching from under the ground. Then finally, when my time was nearly up, in the quietest of voices, I heard one single word coming from somewhere far away. One last word, pregnant with meaning, gasped out along with a death rattle. I turned the word over and over in my mind and pondered what it might have meant. What legacy it had tried to leave with me. I wondered if meaning was something that could even be found. Then the silence became suddenly much deeper.

E is for Environment

I saw the last five minutes of the human race. We had lasted so long, somehow. We had found a way to live despite our own hubris and continue to infest the world with generation after generation of our spawn. It happened very slowly, and then, very suddenly. The environment turned upon us, the Earth trying to kill us back. New diseases ran rampant, plants became toxic, animals began to maul us. Now, we walked among homes that had been overtaken by vines, doors rotting off their hinges as foxes and birds picked through the wreckage to find food and treasures. A pristine Eden without the poison of humankind in its midst killing everything at the root. The air had begun to clean itself again, finally. Our monuments were crumbling to dust. There were so few people left, language itself was no longer relevant, and the sounds in this new paradise did not include those of human beings among them. The others must have slowly died off in all these places where the grasses grew tall and the rain smelled fresh and clean. The last people were sitting in the desert, a tent of simple fabric over their heads to keep the sun from baking them. They were covered in pox, red-faced and wheezing. Small piles of rocks served as graves, evidence that there had once been more of them, but now, these last two held hands, gasping for breath. They lay their heads together, their breathing in sync, and then they shared a leaf between them, tearing it in half with blackened teeth and chewing it into a paste. In. Out. In. Out. Their chests rose and fell as one. A small, orange desert fox cautiously slunk up to the tent and peered in. These two strange creatures were no threat. The fox licked its paws and waited patiently, until as one, the two chests rose no more. The fox and its children would feast like kings tonight.

I saw the last five minutes of the human race. We had lasted so long, somehow. We had found a way to live, despite our own hubris, and continue to infest the world with generation after generation of our spawn. It happened very slowly, and then, very suddenly. The environment turned upon us, the Earth trying to kill us back. New diseases ran rampant, plants became toxic, animals began to maul us. Now, we walked among homes that had been overtaken by vines, doors rotting off their hinges as foxes and birds picked through the wreckage to find food and treasures. A pristine Eden, without the poison of humankind in its midst, killing everything at the root.
The air had begun to clean itself again, finally. Our monuments were crumbling to dust. There were so few people left, language itself was no longer relevant, and the sounds in this new paradise did not include those of human beings among them. The others must have slowly died off in all these places, where the grasses grew tall and the rain smelled fresh and clean. The last people were sitting in the desert, a tent of simple fabric over their heads to keep the sun from baking them. They were covered in pox, red-faced and wheezing. Small piles of rocks served as graves, evidence that there had once been more of them, but now, these last two held hands, gasping for breath.
They lay their heads together, their breathing in sync, and then they shared a leaf between them, tearing it in half with blackened teeth, and chewing it into a paste. In. Out. In. Out. Their chests rose and fell as one. A small, orange, desert fox cautiously slunk up to the tent and peered in. These two strange creatures were no threat. The fox licked its paws and waited patiently, until as one, the two chests rose no more.

F is for Fungi

I saw the last five minutes of the human race. The world had cooled, perhaps the beginning of another ice age, perhaps only another result of irreversible climate change. As in ages past, harkening back to 400 million years ago, long before we infested the planet, fungal blooms had grown large. Twenty-four feet high and nearly a meter across, they towered over the other flora. Typically, for eons, spores died at the internal temperature of human beings, causing us to be at odds with the mushrooms, evolutionarily speaking. Over the past few hundred years, though, our internal body temperatures had been lowering, our evolution continuing toward hyper-hygiene and cleaner environments. Our bodies no longer had to fight bacteria, viruses, and fungal infections as we had in the past. We had eliminated so many of the challenges to our immune systems, and they became slovenly and lazy. As this happened in our species, certain strains of fungi continued to evolve as well, to the point where they could survive at our new internal temperature and thrive. The microbes invaded health-care systems. These new fungi resisted treatment by the few drugs that could be used against them. They thrived on cold hard surfaces and laughed at cleaning chemicals. They caused fast-spreading outbreaks and killed up to two thirds of the people exposed to them. We became catastrophically ill, consigned to intensive care: pharmaceutically paralyzed, plugged into ventilators, threaded with IV lines, loaded with drugs to suppress infection and inflammation. This new, dominant kingdom grew too fast. Our lungs filled with spores, which we breathed in and out, more mushroom than human by the end of our diminishing lives, allowing our killer to spread and grow. I thought back to when I had enjoyed eating mushrooms in the past and wondered at what moment we had become the food.

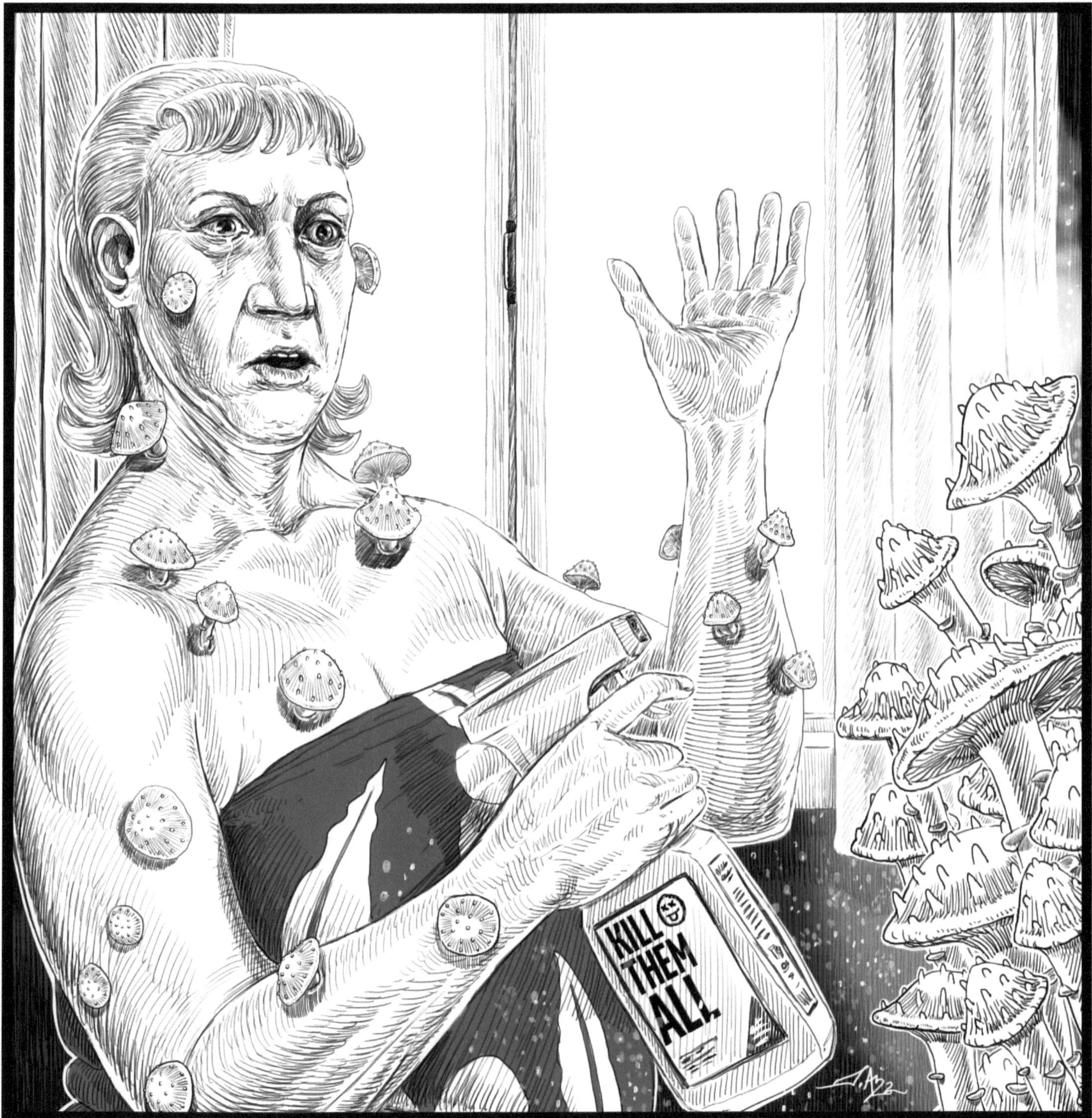

KILL
THEM
AL!

G is for Game

I saw the last five minutes of the human race. We were all simply pieces in a **game**, the size of which was unfathomable. We didn't understand the rules, but from my place outside of time, I could see that there were giant, unknowable hands moving us around the field of play, rolling dice the size of galaxies, putting cards down that appeared to us like the sunrise and sunset, blanketing the entire sky with colors and tones. The game was complex and involved billions of individual pieces, each subject to different rules, moving at different rates and in different directions. What we could never know from our tiny perspective on the game board was that there was a vast array allied against us, pieces like us, only shadows of the reality we knew. The game went back and forth, over and over, endlessly cycling between victory and defeat. Then, finally, whatever mysterious force compelled us to move paused. It became clear that we were losing. Nobody but me saw it coming, as the entity responsible for our side's efforts reared back and howled in frustration. Nobody could have anticipated it flipping the table and storming away, and as we disappeared into the cosmos, we wondered if there was any rule in play by which we could take back our moves and try again.

H is for Hijacked

I saw the last five minutes of the human race. Someone had finally built a space elevator. Once banished to the realm of science-fiction, now it stood on terra firma, extending into space. My first thought was that we had come together and found a way to reach out, to conquer the stars, to explore the boundless reaches of the universe. But then, I noticed all the pirate hats, the jolly roger flying over the capitol buildings, the peg-legs, hook-hands, and eye-patches. These were no ordinary pirates. These were space pirates. They had sailed up in their cosmic galleon and swung over on ropes of stardust, putting our warriors to the sword and securing our treasures for themselves. Though their spoken language was alien to us, those of us who had read pirate stories knew that we had been hijacked. Looking again at the towering monument that led to the stars, I saw a line of insects marching up, defying gravity, an endless line moving up, up, and away. Upon closer inspection, these were not insects after all—they were us. Tied at the wrists, mewling and simpering, asking for mercy. Alien pirates poked us in the backs with their rapiers if we faltered. Earth was no longer our ship. We were being made to walk the plank. As we floated into the endless sea of black above us, it was hard to laugh at the "yarr" sounds raised up like a song all around.

I is for Indifference

I saw the last five minutes of the human race. Something opened up in the sky. A doorway, made of pure geometry, jutting out at unnatural angles in colors and frequencies we couldn't detect with our own feeble senses. Something came through it, something more vast than the sky itself, something that emanated pure waves of pain and madness. At first, we were terrified beyond sanity, sure that this was what all the horror stories had been warning us about. These monsters were here to destroy us all, to make slaves of us, to watch our cities burn and our societies crumble. But, that kind of attention from entities beyond the stars was what we'd spent so much time preparing for. We had not prepared ourselves adequately for the reality. We were beneath their notice. Everything we had built, everything we were was so minimal to their reality that we were less than nothing. The existential dread of a sentience that viewed us with such **indifference** was the true horror. We tried to give ourselves comfort by comparing ourselves to ants being stepped over by careless humans strolling down a sidewalk, but that was an inaccurate comparison. It would have been closer to say that the entire timeline of human experience was one single ant and they were still the expanding universe with no terminus in sight. They obliterated us without ever knowing there was anything there, not even the dust from which we came.

J is for Jogging

I saw the last five minutes of the human race. It seemed like a good thing that we had taken a long, hard look at ourselves in the mirror. Humanity was growing fat, slovenly, ugly, with labored breathing and preventable health problems plaguing even the most stalwart individual. Somehow, we came together, and with the help of some particularly influential trend-setters, everyone started jogging. Gym memberships were skyrocketing, and pollution declined as fewer and fewer people used cars to get to work or school. Laziness was no longer seen as a reward for the rich nor as an affliction of the idle—it was simply toxic. The trend shot upward, breaking records and subverting eons of evolution, as humans began to care about their health. Jogging clubs formed, at first just among friends who enjoyed spending time in the fresh air together, but these groups grew, and soon entire jogging gangs coalesced. Turf wars were next, with malls being taken over by gangs of jogging seniors and school tracks fiercely guarded by junior varsity basketball teams. Jogging shoes became weaponized, as there was only so much room on the sidewalks, and the idea that a stranger might keep you from jogging was simply absurd to any sane person. Like the ancient horrors of death dancing or ergot poisoning, but for health, jogging surpassed all other needs, and we kept running. We ran until our feet began to bleed, the skin calloused and sloughing off, our toes growing together for greater stability. We forced our own biological evolution to catch up as we ran on ahead, faster and with greater urgency. The weak among us died, but those who lived grew sleek and wind-resistant, turning into blurs of angry, healthy energy. Nobody remembered what we had started running from or running for in those final days, but that no longer mattered. Fitness was paramount, next to godliness, and perhaps even racing past that in the grand scheme of human ambition.

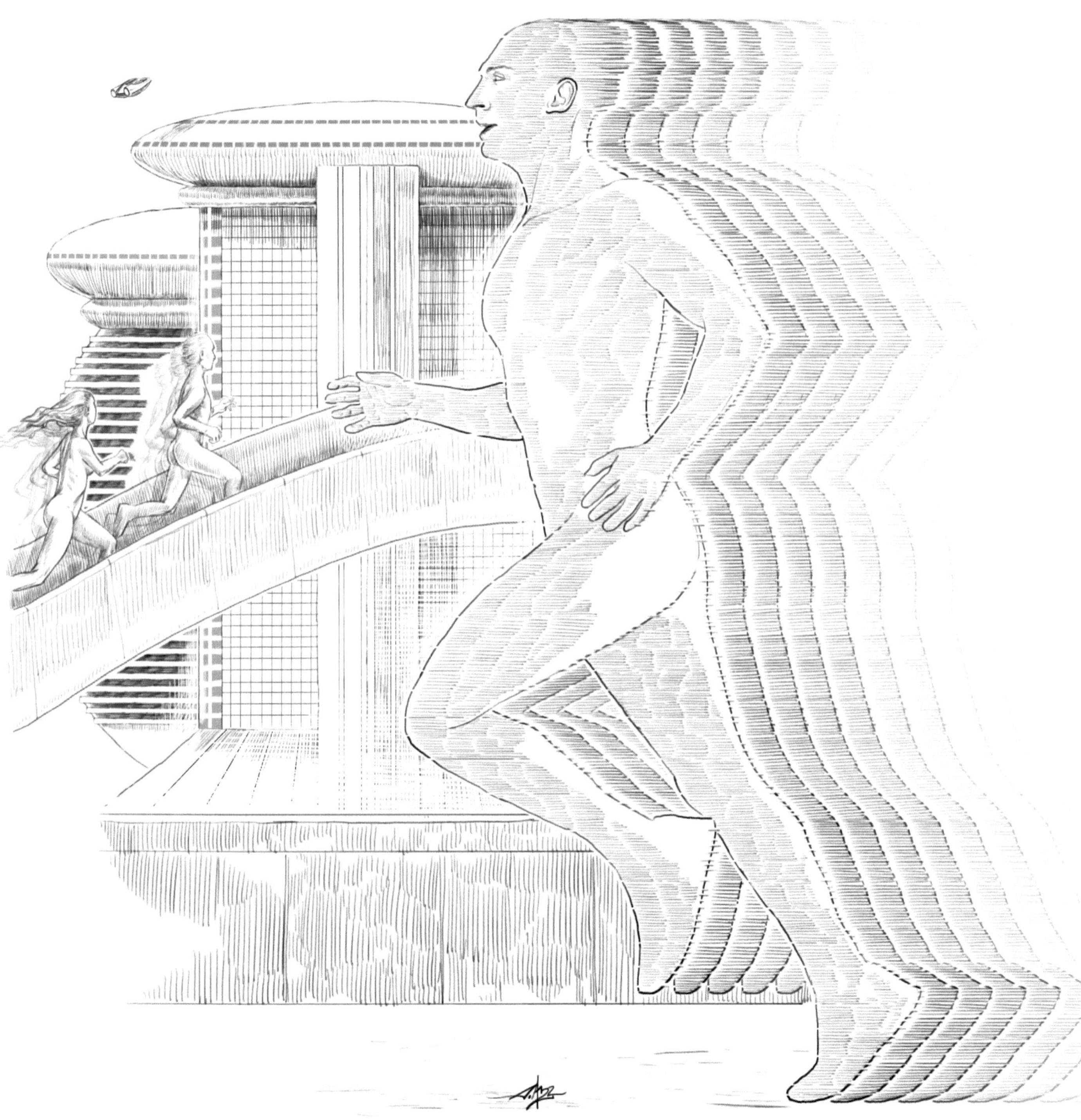

K is for Kaiju

I saw the last five minutes of the human race. The Japanese called them kaiju. It translates to "strange beast" in their language but had become, by this time, an almost universal loan word. The Japanese did not have exclusive access to giant, destructive monsters. Every culture on Earth had its own legends and myths containing multitudes. Giant apes crawling up the sides of buildings. Massive quivering blobs so enormous they engulf entire Pacific islands. Reptilian scourges that breathe fire and burn the countryside. Flying creatures whose massive wingspans blot out the sun and smash buildings into pulp. Undersea leviathans surfacing long enough to gulp down entire beach towns, leaving nothing but scorched sand dunes. Fanged thunder lizards, long thought extinct, chewing their way across the savannah, gulping down anything smaller. Bulletproof shelled giants rocketing through the sky and bringing down planes in the wake of their blazing jet stream. We all knew the legends—everyone had one—but nobody expected that they were all very real, or that they would all show up at the same time, or that they had lain in wait for eons, dancing at the edge of our senses, ensuring they were observed in dreams as fiction until they could strike. Villages eaten, cities destroyed, the sky burned with radiation and the screams of angry monsters. Our weapons were useless, and they proved, in the end, that despite our hubris, the Earth was never ours to begin with.

L is for Life

I saw the last five minutes of the human race. The world was no longer recognizable. Human beings were no more present in this epoch than the earliest of the dinosaurs. Earth was millions of years beyond our pathetic timeline. Humankind and all its history had been a blip, as insignificant as a speck on a lens. Another race had risen up to take our place, something else entirely. These creatures were silicon based, totally unlike the carbon based life-forms we had thought were the only possible expression of life. We would not have recognized them as life with our child-like understanding of the vast universe. They, in turn, did not recognize us as such either. I watched some form of archeological dig. These beings of shifting rock, chemical impulses, senses that were different from any I had experienced. Beneath the soil, far under long dormant volcanic rock, they toiled, moving piles of matter around, and that was when I saw them uncover human remains. Only the faintest trace of a fossil, a human skull, I knew it like it was my own. Maybe it was? Somehow, this last piece of what we had been survived, preserved in a state beyond ashes and dust. They appraised it, understanding it somehow on some level, and then, not recognizing the last piece of what we had been as a significant find, tossed it over among the other rocks, where it was crushed beneath the growing pile of refuse. They were looking for something important, and it was not us.

M is for Machines

I saw the last five minutes of the human race. I was in a gleaming city with towers all around me. I saw no other humans, just **machines**. Machines flying through the sky, rolling over desiccated earth, projecting light. I couldn't read the language on any of the surfaces, although some of the characters looked familiar. I recognized an A and a U and an X. The number system was no longer the familiar base 10 system, covering many surfaces with bizarre symbols and codes, and I saw walls with units of measurement I did not understand. The sky was a different shade of blue than I was used to. Where the humans were, I couldn't say. Society seemed to be running itself without our interference. Everything was automated. I saw nothing I recognized as human, just the interminable, quiet hum of machines doing their endless tasks, interacting with one another, a perpetual motion machine of our own creation with too many moving parts to even begin to understand. The machines had no reason for foresight. They had no existential questions. Even if they knew that the sun had exploded seven and a half minutes before, why would they care? There was nothing to do, so they kept doing their work, right up to the moment when, in one blazing millisecond, a flash of light burst over everything and the sun swallowed up our history, our civilizations, our cellular structure, and then, I was alone in space, surrounded by the absence of matter; the void, all that remained.

N is for Nyotaimori

I saw the last five minutes of the human race. My view tilts upward from the empty, barren streets, ascending through the window of a condo building. Beautiful scarlet curtains frame a sturdy double-paned window, now cracked open just a touch to allow some breeze into the warm and cozy living room. I find myself at the back of a line of people. I immediately feel underdressed, even though I am not inside a body, clothed only in a lingering sense of anxious self-loathing. Everyone else looks amazing, thrown together in effortless looks that take an immense amount of effort in the way that only the rich have mastered. Ahead, the line deposits people before a table with long, pristine, elegant runners floating in every direction. I can see glimpses of flesh through the crowd, ivory skin dotted with delicate pink features. A naked woman. A **Nyotaimori** ceremony, the traditional Japanese body sushi experience. I see people walking away, smiling, a solemn looking chef watching over the line, placing ultra-thin slices of meat like Jamon Iberico on beds of greenery, vegetables serving more as color than nutrition. One by one, the line empties as the diners shuffle forward, bowing their heads in silence but making tiny whimpering sounds of anticipation, glistening meat on hungry minds. The crowd thins, and my eyes follow the curve of the woman's body, from eyes closed in silent repose, down the curve of her neck and over supple breasts, and down to the sine wave of her hips. My mouth unable to speak, my eyes unable to close, I observe the chef taking a long knife and delicately slicing into the dead woman's leg, cutting the thinnest, almost transparent layer from the muscle. Below her waist, she has been flayed open, butchered, and I realize that she is not asleep at all. There is no sense of the taboo in this place. This is not a crime or anathema. The thing we clung to, which separated us from the animals, that wall has been breached. We devour the flesh of our own. I cannot turn away as I watch this woman devoured, and I reflect on how this must have begun and the inevitable decline that led to this place where we can no longer call ourselves humans. The blood dribbles down the necks and chins of the assembled, and I wish I had eyes to weep.

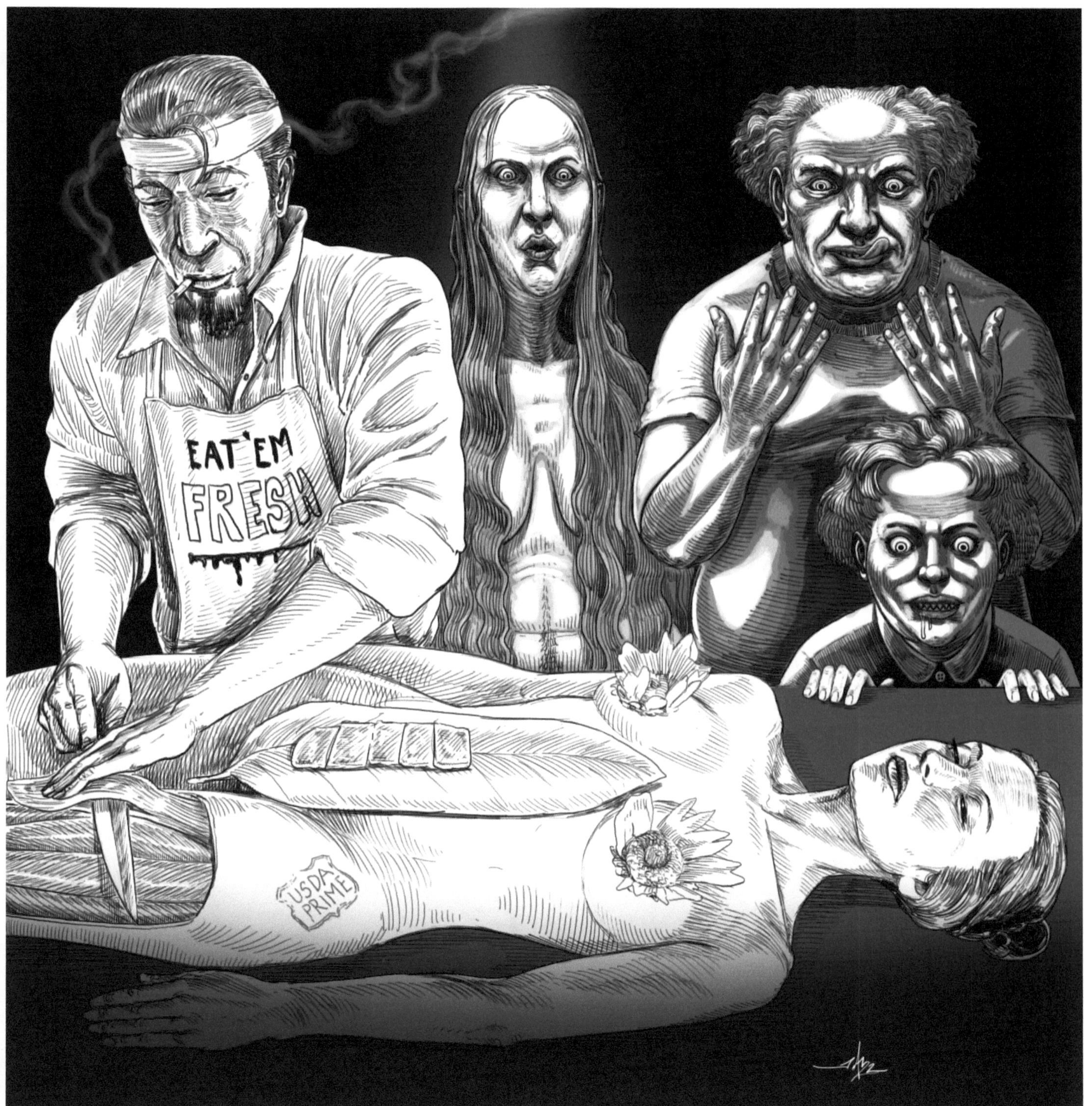
EAT'EM
FRESH
USDA
PRIME

O is for Ocean

I saw the last five minutes of the human race. Climate change had turned the once majestic polar ice caps into little more than whiskey cubes for a highball. Oxygen levels were becoming lower, forcing our bodies to learn to breathe differently to survive. Little did we know this would be necessary in the times to come. Our moment of truth was gradual, then sudden, with tsunamis and storms overtaking our shores and smashing our pathetic human creations to rubble. But our mother, the ocean? She had not abandoned us. Countless millennia ago, we had exited the waters, vowing never to return, leaving our gills behind for lungs, shedding our fins for limbs, but as prodigal as we were, she had not forgotten her children. The ocean grew, and the land shrank away, a vestige of a lost age. Where once deserts baked in the harsh sun, tropical fish began to swim. Our gasping, flailing attempts at living in this new paradise were destined for failure. Deaths on an unprecedented scale. And yet, slowly, inevitably, there were survivors and newborn lungs that had learned in the womb how to take in oxygen from the sea. Our diets changed along with the tides as we embraced our heritage and became creatures of the water. Legs began to fuse, and toes grew webbing between them to help propel us through this nascent biome as our ancient progenitor embraced us. The waves, crashing against the few rocks able to stand above the surface, seemed to whisper, "welcome home, children," as we embodied our mermaid legends and evolved to start again down in the depths beyond.

I saw the last five minutes of the human race. Climate change had turned the once majestic polar ice caps into little more than whiskey cubes for a highball. Oxygen levels were becoming lower, forcing our bodies to learn to breathe differently to survive. Little did we know this would be necessary in the times to come. Our moment of truth was gradual, then sudden, with tsunamis and storms overtaking our shores and smashing our pathetic human creations to rubble. But our mother, the ocean? She had not abandoned us. Countless millennia ago, we had exited the waters, vowing never to return, leaving our gills behind for lungs, shedding our fins for limbs, but as prodigal as we were, she had not forgotten her children. The ocean grew, and the land shrank away, a vestige of a lost age. Where once deserts baked in the harsh sun, tropical fish began to swim. Our gasping, flailing attempts at living in this new paradise were destined for failure. Deaths on an unprecedented scale. And yet, slowly, there were survivors and newborn lungs that had learned in the womb how to take in oxygen from the sea. Our diets changed along with the tides as we embraced our heritage and became creatures of the water. Legs began to fuse, and toes grew webbing between them to help propel us through this nascent biome as our ancient progenitor embraced us. The waves, crashing against the few rocks able to stand above the surface, seemed to whisper, "welcome home, children," as we embodied our mermaid legends and evolved to start again down in the depths beyond.

P is for Pandemic

I saw the last five minutes of the human race. Another pandemic, another botched response. The air was thick with the virus, a super-spreader, conveniently transmissible through the water, the air, droplets, breaths. All human contact was suspect. Nobody could agree about how to fight it or what measures needed to be put into place to stop it. History repeated itself again and again, but instead of rolling the dice and coming up lucky, this time, the human race failed. This time, there was no final act yet to come. In these last five minutes, the viral load was greater than the ants, the beetles, the birds, and even all the bacteria that made up the ecosystem we called the human body. The virus was omnipresent, replicating itself as we argued and debated, until there were no hosts left to infect. Spreading and reproducing until the very environment that sustained it was dead, unable to contain any more, unable to sustain its inevitable growth. I couldn't help but reflect on the irony of this as the last humans took their last, dying breaths through perforated lungs.

I saw the last five minutes of the human race. Another pandemic, another botched response. The air was thick with the virus, a super-spreader, conveniatly transmissible through the water, the air, droplets, breaths. All human contact was suspect. Nobody could agree about how to fight it or what measures needed to be put into place to stop it. History repeated itself again and again, but instead of rolling the dice and coming up lucky, this time, the human race failed. This time, there was no final act yet to come. In these last five minutes, the viral load was greater than the ants, the beetles, the birds, and even all the bacteria that made up the ecosystem we called the human body. The virus was omnipresent, replicating itself as we argued and debated, until there were no hosts left to infect. Spreading and reproducing until the very environment that sustained it was dead, unable to contain any more, unable to sustain it's inevitable growth. I couldn't help but reflect on the irony of this as the last humans took their last, dying breaths through perforated lungs.

Q is for Questions

I saw the last five minutes of the human race. I was in heaven, looking down at the Earth from a fluffy cloud. Next to me, God stood, so bright I couldn't look at his face, so tall that I only reached his ankles. I felt things winding down, and I turned to God, knowing that chances like this were few and far between. I asked if he would mind, and he said "no," so I began to ask God questions. "Why is there suffering in the world? Why are good people hurt, and why are evil people allowed to thrive? Is free will possible, or are we destined to follow the path set before us? Why is everything so filled with fear, sadness, and anger? How can we be happy? What can we do?" God stood for a moment and thought as I waited for the answers. His voice cracked with barely controlled panic as he knelt beside me and put his giant hands together. "Good questions! Let's pray about it!" God began to mumble, making frantic gyrations and exaltations. "Oh great one, mysterious force, why am I here? Where did I come from? What is the meaning of all this?" I watched God talk to ghosts, and he seemed so much smaller somehow than when we'd begun.

R is for Rapture

I saw the last five minutes of the human race. People floated above the ground, but only about one in ten. They were bathed in a radiant light, awash with a glow that blinded those around them. The rapture had come, only when I looked closer, there was no rhyme or reason to who was chosen. There were a few devout Christians, a few Orthodox Jews, some Satanists, a Buddhist monk, and numerous atheists in my neighborhood alone. There were some cats, some dogs, and a gopher. Ten percent of a colony of ants floated above their hill while the rest of the colony frantically sent signals, wondering how to get their brethren back down. Some people prayed. Some laughed. Some looked scared. One threw up, looking like he was suffering from vertigo. Then, they all began to float away, up into the sky. We watched from Earth as they rose higher and higher until, finally, they disappeared into the upper layers of the atmosphere. This took just under five minutes, and a sudden flash of light after the last of them had vanished into the cosmos told me all I needed to know.

S is for Strings

I saw the last five minutes of the human race. I had never noticed before that every single living being had **strings** attached, stretching far up into the sky and disappearing into the black. Everyone's limbs were being puppeted by some unseen force from above. Their mouths opened and closed on hinges. We went about our business like characters in a farce. The poetry of human movement, the dance of life, seemed suddenly diminished, wooden and imprecise. I wondered why I had never seen the strings. They seemed so obvious, so painfully visible. Our systems were a series of ropes and gizmos, pushed and pulled, and our choices were being made for us. Then, without warning, the strings all dropped by the billions, crashing to the surface around us, cut off from the heavens. People dropped where they stood, never to move again. We had finally been abandoned by the puppeteer.

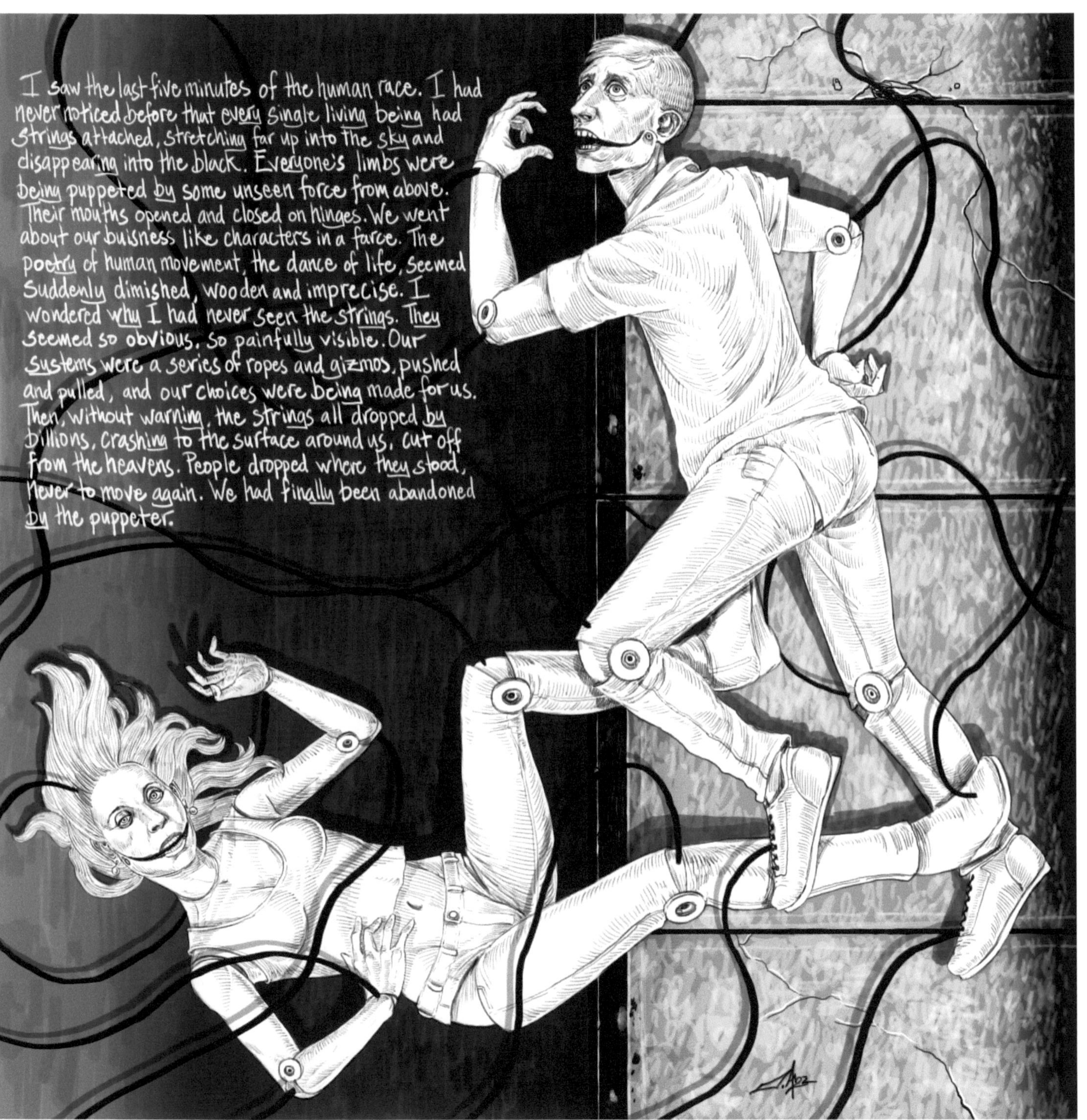

I saw the last five minutes of the human race. I had never noticed before that every single living being had strings attached, stretching far up into the sky and disappearing into the black. Everyone's limbs were being puppeted by some unseen force from above. Their mouths opened and closed on hinges. We went about our buisness like characters in a farce. The poetry of human movement, the dance of life, seemed suddenly dimished, wooden and imprecise. I wondered why I had never seen the strings. They seemed so obvious, so painfully visible. Our systems were a series of ropes and gizmos, pushed and pulled, and our choices were being made for us. Then, without warning, the strings all dropped by billions, crashing to the surface around us, cut off from the heavens. People dropped where they stood, never to move again. We had finally been abandoned by the puppeter.

T is for Time

I saw the last five minutes of the human race. I finally took the plunge and traveled through time. Once discovered, time travel became a hobby, then a fad, and finally, an obsession. It developed and grew until it was almost impossible to find anyone who hadn't tried it. The issue with this was that it was only possible to go forward in time, never backward. There were no do-overs and no way to go back and fix mistakes made in the past. The past was concrete, only the future was fluid. There was a sense of loss when friends and family took their journey. Suddenly, we found ourselves without them in the present. It was pointed out to those who remained skeptical that if everyone leaped ahead, we would all be together again there in the future. There was no need for the grief of loss. We would simply meet again in some other year, far away. Once this opinion had spread, the whole endeavor was bathed in a more positive light. It replaced the nebulous hope we'd once had of being with our dead loved ones again in some afterlife with the very real fact that we would be with them throughout time, seeing wonders to come and understanding more about the nature of being together. I arrived, already grinning, excited to see who would greet me. Stretching out in a long trail, floating silently: an endless series of dead astronauts. Skeletons, suspended in space, creating an asteroid belt of frozen meat. In our hubris, we had neglected to account for time and space being eternally entwined and left a vast orbit of our dead behind a planet that was no longer where it had been when we left. As my body froze, as the oxygen leaked out of my aching lungs, as my eyes went glassy and iced over, I looked into the hollow sockets of some other explorer, knowing that I'd soon become the welcoming committee for the next person to realize their terrible mistake.

U is for Upload

I saw the last five minutes of the human race. The upload was almost complete. This event was the culmination of one carried out billions of times before. Many of the earliest attempts had ended in terrible tragedy. The loss of life was tremendous. People protested and fought at first, the idea being anathema to the human experience. How could we possibly remain human beings if our thoughts came from processors and quantum computers? Early adapters pointed out that historically, the thing that made us "us" was a series of electrical signals firing off between neurons and synapses in a large piece of liquid-suspended meat, sitting atop a mobile cage of bones, connected with yet more meat. This was not so different from putting those same signals through a series of metal, silicon, and wire. Being in a more physically resilient shell and less in need of resources would allow us, essentially, to live forever. It took generations for the idea to become normalized, going from a radical transhumanist experiment to a fetish, to a fad, to a progressive cause, and, finally, to a mainstream idea. Beyond that, as the numbers of detractors diminished, it moved into the territory of something only people on the fringes would turn down, anti-science lunatics and trouble-makers. Years after that, it became mandatory as resources shrunk and population levels continued to explode. This person was the last, surrounded by family, already in their shells of synthetic immortality, staring at him, emotions painted on their faces by servos and microscopic motors. He was scared and had held out as long as possible, but now he was the last thing keeping humanity from ascending to their next form. An obsolete bag of flesh and blood that would someday end, no matter what he did. As his blood drained through the tube into a complex cleaning machine and his brain began to get fuzzy, his eyes closed as though he was hypnotized. The electrical impulses that made up his thoughts and feelings and love and hate were converted into an incredible series of 1s and 0s, all flowing into his new, solid-state drive. From organic to synthetic. What was really "him" in those moments where he lived between the two containers, it is impossible to say.

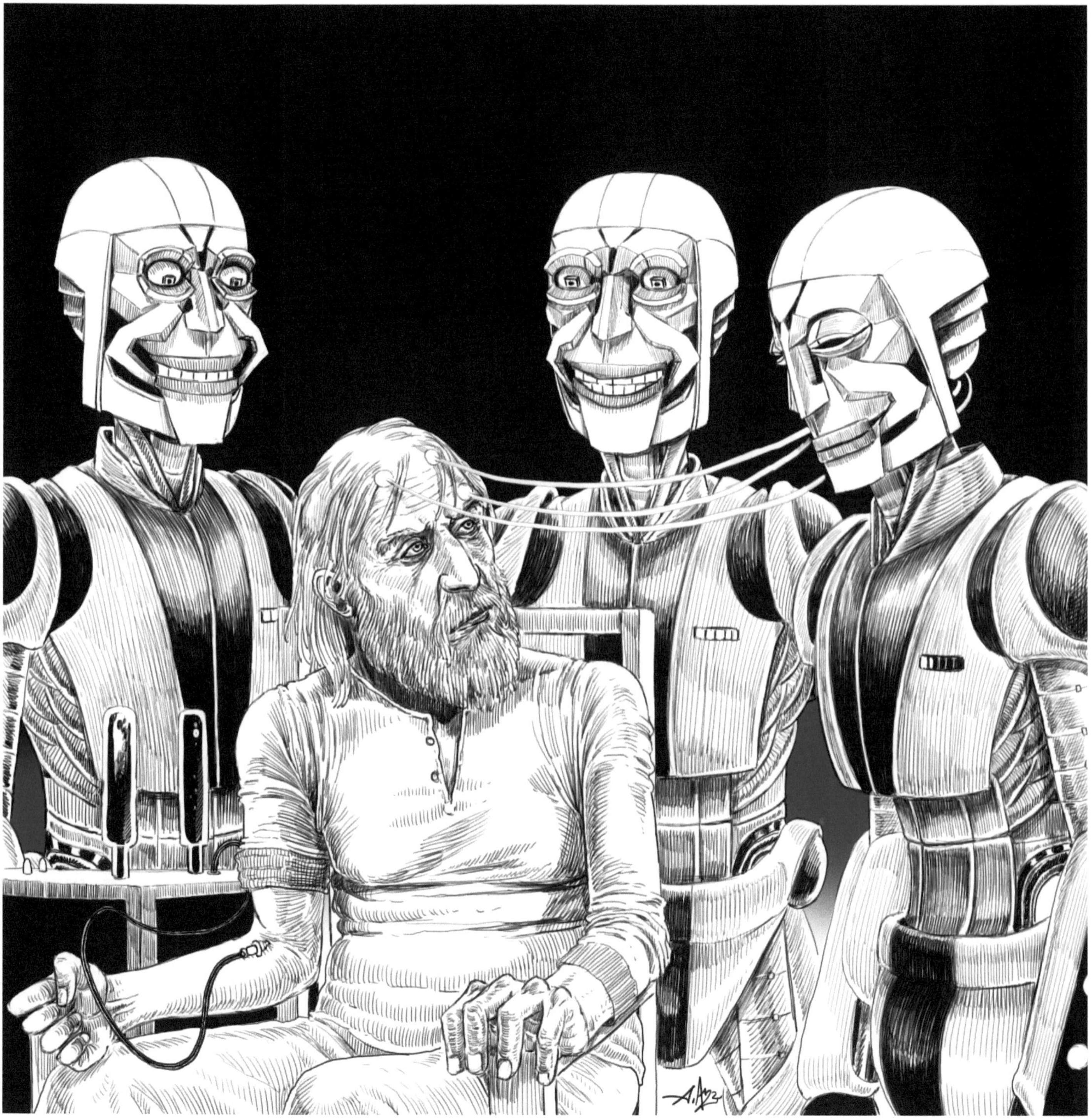

V is for Vacation

I saw the last five minutes of the human race. I wandered around like a confused toddler watching parents prepare for something beyond my understanding. Things were happening too fast to process. Every person I saw was packing their belongings. Suitcases, briefcases, rucksacks, bindles, guitar cases, toolboxes, tackle boxes, gym bags, and shopping carts littered the landscape, stuffed to the brim with merchandise. It was a museum of capitalist excess. The poorest of the poor gathered their meager belongings into scavenged paper bags, and they stood next to rich people, resplendent in their finery, pulling expensive wheeled cases with intricate locks. The strangest thing about all of this was that nobody appeared to be unhappy. Where I expected riots and brawls, there were only people offering each other candy, making small talk, smiling politely, or playing games as they queued up in impossibly long lines. Nobody was driving vehicles, no planes were in the sky, all the boats remained docked at the harbors, and public transit had vanished after all subway cars and el trains ground to a halt at their termini. I was stuck outside of time, unable to speak with these people, and so I could only watch as the lines stretched into the horizon. Then, as though driven by some unseen signal lamp, the lines began to move. I traveled toward the front of the line, trying to understand the mystery. Hawaiian shirts and Panama hats, comfy sweatpants and cargo shorts, sunglasses and tank tops–the majority were dressed like they were going on vacation. At the front of the line, a portal was open, swirling cerulean blue. As the line of travelers crossed the threshold, they blinked out of existence. I tried to follow, but just as I was immaterial to the human race, so was I unable to touch the magic for myself, and slowly, inevitably, the human race left on their getaway. I wondered where everyone had decided to go. I wondered if they would need sunscreen. I wondered who would get their mail for them, but that was ridiculous. There would be no mail. There would be no television. There would be no lunches at inner city delis with great corned beef sandwiches. There would be no more of anything we'd made. I'd taken it all for granted. It was just hard to accept that everyone had gone on vacation without me. I wondered if they would bring back souvenirs. And finally, I wondered if there was any way for me to follow... because the loneliness was already setting in.

W is for Wish

I saw the last five minutes of the human race. I made a **wish**. I was absolutely sure my wish to witness the last five minutes of human existence would come true. Nothing happened. I was still in my own bedroom on the same day, according to my desktop calendar. I was disappointed. Then I glanced at the clock. I had traveled back in time two minutes. I had been very specific with my wish: "Let me see the last five minutes of the human race." Now, I wondered, paralyzed, what I would do with my last three minutes. I stood there, perfectly still, without the removed distance of metaphors to protect me, unable to stop shaking.

I saw the last five minutes of the human race. I made a wish. I was absolutely sure my wish to witness the last five minutes of human existence would come true. Nothing happened. I was still in my own bedroom on the same day, according to my desktop calender. I was disappointed. Then I glanced at the clock. I had traveled back in time two minutes. I had been very specific with my wish: "Let me see the last five minutes of the human race." Now, I wondered, paralyzed, what I would do with my last three minutes. I stood there, perfectly still, without the removed distance of metaphors to protect me, unable to stop shaking.

X is for X-Rays

I saw the last five minutes of the human race. **X-Rays** flashed through the air, invisible but deadly, shredding our cells to ribbons, blossoming cancer, boiling us in our own blood. The same phenomena we had harnessed to heat our microwave burritos now cooked the atmosphere. A great extinction. I thought about the time, as a teenager, I put a penny in a microwave, just to see what might happen, and watched as it sparked and spewed and smoked, ruining the device and starting a tiny radioactive fire. I wondered what we had done to unleash this, whether cosmic rays had decided we were done here or whether we had done something to ourselves. The odds were good. I watched a pile of screaming people burning alive. The smell was indescribable. The explosions were much harder to watch than the penny had been.

Y is for Yearning

I saw the last five minutes of the human race. A female stood, dressed in a piece of clothing that lashed around her, protecting her from the elements. She looked desperate, old, aged before her time. I saw something like people pass around her, walking somewhere, a long line of humans, but they weren't human. At every great evolutionary divergence, there was one domino at the tipping point, one egg that, when hatched, was now a chicken but had not been laid by a chicken. One ape that was now a ground-dweller who would no longer go back to the trees. At the same time, at the other end, there was the one fish that was unable to evolve legs, the one single cell that couldn't split into two and become more complex. An evolutionary dead end. A period on the sentence of a lineage. This female tried to communicate with the long line of humans, but they couldn't understand her. She made sounds, and they just glanced over, eyes wide, confused about her attempts. A great yearning rose within her. She remembered that there once were things like her, perhaps many years ago, but now there were none. They had all moved on without her, and now she was alone.

Z is for Zephyr

I saw the last five minutes of the human race, and it was the most beautiful and terrifying thing I could imagine. I stood among heroes, gazing through the blackness of space at the Earth far below us. Sound didn't exist here but for our breathing, each person lost in the echoes of their own continued existence. There were a dozen or so in this room of various races and genders and nationalities, all connected by this mission they had taken upon themselves. It was a station of hundreds, and every window was surrounded by a group of shocked individuals watching as it began. The explosions were so large and so numerous that the surface of the planet broke out in hives. Cracks began to appear, and slowly, they widened until they were unmistakable even from this distance. The Earth was gone, and with it, all its creatures and resources. The existential horror at being the only humans left sunk in like concrete blocks thrown into a cold lake. Here, on this station, there were ships. There were grow houses and breeding experiments with animals. There were ways to move around the solar system like tiny specks of dust blown about in a maelstrom. But there would be no return home. No resupply or staff rotation or even letters from those back on Earth for these creatures, floating now without anchor, the remains of an orphaned species from a place now only a statistic in the history of the universe. Humans had been born of Earth, the entire history of the life-form tied intrinsically to the mud and dust from which it came. Now, for the first time since creation, human beings had no home planet. They looked around at each other and wordlessly began to come together, holding one another for comfort that needed no words. Words would come, but this was not yet the time. The station was called Zephyr, after the Greek word meaning a soft, gentle breeze. It had never felt so apt now that they were like leaves blowing from their tree. I wondered how they might die, this being the last five minutes of humanity, but they didn't die. They made the choice not to die. Something in their eyes changed as they came to realize, one by one, they would survive. They would make children. They would try to thrive despite all odds. They had to. No child had ever been born in space. None had been conceived here. Things would inevitably be different. How would we evolve? What might we become? These creatures would no longer be human, they would have to become something else. The path of humans ended here, leaving their origins behind just as children leave their parents to go out into the chaos and become something new. The path ahead was dark, twisting, and filled with endless, eternal potential. And in that moment, I understood that not all endings are opposed to beginnings.

I saw the last five minutes of the human race, and it was beautiful and terrifying thing I could imgine. I stood among heroes, gazing through the blackness of space at the Earth below us. Sound didn't exist here but for our breathing, each person lost in the echoes of their own continued existence. There were a dozen or so in this room of various races and genders and nationalities, all connected by this mission they had taken upon themselves. It was a station of hundreds, and every window was surrounded by a group of shocked individuals watching as it began. The explosions were so large and numerous the surface of the planet broke out in hives. Cracks began to appear, and slowly, they widened until they were unmistakable even from this distance. The Earth was gone, and with it, all it's creatures and resources. The existential horror at being the only humans left sunk in like concrete blocks thrown into a cold lake. Here, on this station, there were ships. There were grow houses and breeding experiments with animals. There were ways to move around the solar system like tiny specks of dust blown about in a maelstrom. But there would be no return home. No resupply or staff rotation or even letters from those back on Earth for these creatures, floating now without anchor, the remains of an

orphaned species from a place now only a statistic in the history of the universe. Humans had been born of Earth, the entire history of the life-form tied intrinsically to the mud and dust from which it came. Now, for the first time since creation, human beings had no home planet. They looked around at each other and wordlessly began to come together, holding one another for comfort that needed no words. Words would come, but this was not yet the time. The station was called Zephyr, after the Greek word meaning a soft, gentle breeze. It had never felt so apt now they were like leaves blowing from their tree. I wondered how they might die, this being the last five minutes of humanity, but they didn't die. They made the choice not to die. Something in their eyes changed as they came to realize, one by one, the would survive. They would make children. They would try to thrive despite all odds. They had to. No child had ever been born in space. None had been concieved here. Things would inevitably be different. How would we evolve? What might we become? These creatures would no longer be human, they would have to become something else. The path of humans ended here, leaving their origins behind just as children leave their parents to go out into the chaos and become something new. The path ahead was dark, twisting, and filled with endless, eternal potential. And in that moment, I understood that not all endings are opposed to beginings.

& More...

I saw the last five minutes of the human race. We had always wanted **more**. More money. More sex. More violence. More content. More friends. More power. The human race was a story of excess, greed, and want. We couldn't be satisfied. We wanted success, and we wanted respect, and we wanted property, and, and, and. Our consumption knew no boundaries. On its surface, any transaction was supposed to be balanced carefully between the needs of the involved parties, but in reality, if we zoom in and look at the microscopic rot between the fibers, one side or the other was always trying to put their thumb on the scale and unbalance the load. More. More. More. We wanted this, and that, and those, and these, and the other thing as well. In matters of commerce, in matters of art, even down to the very nature of our own souls, indulgences piled up like gold in a dragon's hoard, until we were laden with the weight of our own corruption. We forgot what it was to be satisfied. One more coin. One more foot of space. One more follower. One more page. One more ink-stained dead tree. One more squeeze of the author's cerebrum. One more splash of ink from the illustrator's pen. We wanted more & more & more & more & ...

& more
& more

Michael Allen Rose is an award winning writer, musician and performer based in Chicago. He has published numerous books and short stories in the bizarro, horror, and comedy arenas, including the recipient of the 2021 Wonderland Award for best bizarro novel, "Jurassichrist." As of 2023, he is the president of the Bizarro Writers Association. Michael also hosts events including the Ultimate Bizarro Showdown, and makes industrial music under the name Flood Damage. He loves cats and a good cup of tea. Find out more about his work at www.michaelallenrose.com

Jim Agpalza was born and raised on an island in the middle of the Pacific. He now resides in Portland Oregon with his wife and two kids and a cat, and a ghost cat. He has spent his whole life drawing the end of the world.

Michael would like to thank John Baltisberger for seeing the potential in this project, despite its dire consequences, Courtney Rader for many existential coffee sessions, some of which inspired entries in this book, and Jim for bringing Michael's terrible prophecies to life via the magic of ink and paper. Jim would like to thank Michael for being such a supportive friend and comrade. Both of them would like to thank the Earth, for putting up with all the bullshit of the human race. We're sorry. Maybe the next dominant lifeform will be better.